Tom Kitten

Retold by
Sarah Toast

Book illustrated by
T. F. Marsh
and
Pat Schoonover

Cover illustrated by
Anita Nelson

Based on the original story by Beatrix Potter with all new illustrations.

Louis Weber, C.E.O.
Publications International, Ltd.
7373 North Cicero Avenue
Lincolnwood, Illinois 60646

Manufactured in U.S.A.

8 7 6 5 4 3 2 1

ISBN: 0-7853-2206-X

PUBLICATIONS INTERNATIONAL, LTD.
Rainbow is a trademark of Publications International, Ltd.

Once upon a time there were three little kittens. Their names were Moppet, Mittens, and Tom Kitten.

Dressed in their own little fur coats, they tumbled and played in the dust near the doorstep.

One day the mother of the kittens, Mrs. Tabitha Twitchit, invited some of her friends to a tea party. Mrs. Tabitha wanted her three kittens to make a fine impression, so she brought them inside to tidy them up and dress them before her friends arrived.

First she scrubbed their faces. Then she brushed their fur and combed their tails and whiskers.

Mrs. Tabitha Twitchit dressed Moppet and Mittens in white dresses with pretty lace kerchiefs around their shoulders. Then she searched through a drawer of dress-up clothes to find something for Tom Kitten to wear.

Tom Kitten had grown. When Mrs. Tabitha put a little blue suit on him, several buttons popped off. She had to sew them on again.

When the three kittens were all dressed, Mrs. Tabitha did a foolish thing. She sent them out to the garden while she made toast for the tea party.

"Keep your good clothes clean! Don't play in the dirt! And keep away from the Puddle-Ducks!" she said.

Moppet and Mittens walked down the garden path unsteadily on their hind legs. Then Moppet tripped and fell on her nose. Mittens did likewise. When they got up, their white dresses were dirty in front.

Moppet said, "Let's sit quietly on the garden wall."

Moppet and Mittens turned their dresses back to front and reached the top of the garden wall with a skip and a jump. But Moppet's fine white lace kerchief fell down into the road.

Tom Kitten tried to join Moppet and Mittens on the garden wall, but he couldn't jump in his tight trousers. He had to climb up the wall rock by rock, breaking ferns and popping buttons right and left.

Tom Kitten's clothes were torn and dirty when he got to the top of the wall. When Moppet and Mittens tried to help him, his hat fell off and the rest of his buttons broke.

Tom wriggled out of his little coat and tight trousers. They fell in a heap in the road.

While Moppet and Mittens were trying to tidy up Tom, there came a pit pat, paddle pat! It came from the three Puddle-Ducks waddling along the road toward them.

As the three Puddle-Ducks marched one behind the other, their webbed feet slapped the road. Pit pat, paddle pat! Pit pat, waddle pat!

Mr. Drake Puddle-Duck and Jemima and Rebecca Puddle-Duck stopped and stood in a row. The three ducks stared at the three kittens on the garden wall. Their eyes were tiny, and they looked surprised.

Jemima and Rebecca picked up Tom Kitten's hat and Moppet's kerchief and put them on.

The kittens all laughed so hard they fell off the wall. Mittens's and Moppet's dresses came off on the way down.

Then Mr. Puddle-Duck waddled over and put on the clothes, though they fit him badly.

"Good day to you!" said Drake Puddle-Duck. The Puddle-Ducks set off up the road, keeping step.

When Mrs. Tabitha Twitchit came looking for her kittens, she found them up on the wall with no clothes on.

Mrs. Tabitha pulled each of the kittens down from the wall. Then she marched them back into the house, scolding all the way.

"My friends will arrive in a few minutes, and the three of you are not even fit to be seen! I am so upset!" said Mrs. Tabitha Twitchit.

She sent the three kittens upstairs. When her friends arrived for the party, Mrs. Tabitha told them that her kittens were in bed with bad colds, which was not true at all.

On the contrary, the kittens were not even in bed. And they didn't stay in their room.

There were some very strange noises from upstairs. The bumping and thumping of the naughty kittens' wild kitten games ruined Mrs. Tabitha's nice tea party.

And somehow, all of the guests' lovely coats and hats, which had been carefully laid on Mrs. Tabitha Twitchit's bed, ended up in a large heap on the bedroom floor.

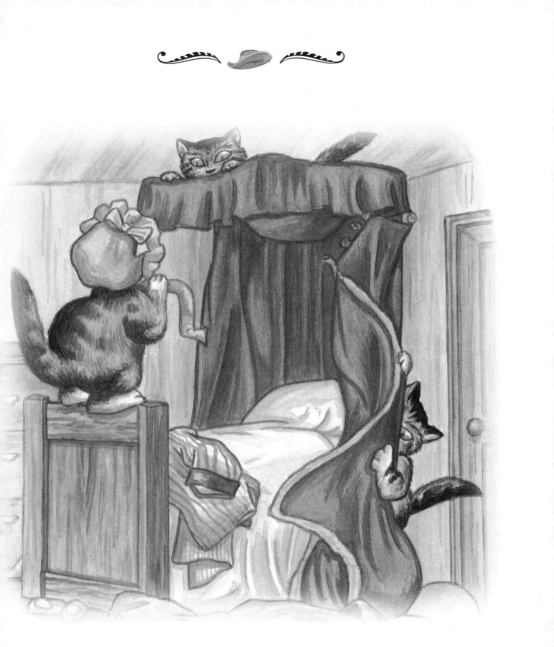

As for the Puddle-Ducks,
they marched to the pond in their fine
new clothes. But the clothes came off
when the ducks jumped in the water.
Mr. Drake Puddle-Duck and Jemima
and Rebecca have been looking for the
clothes ever since.